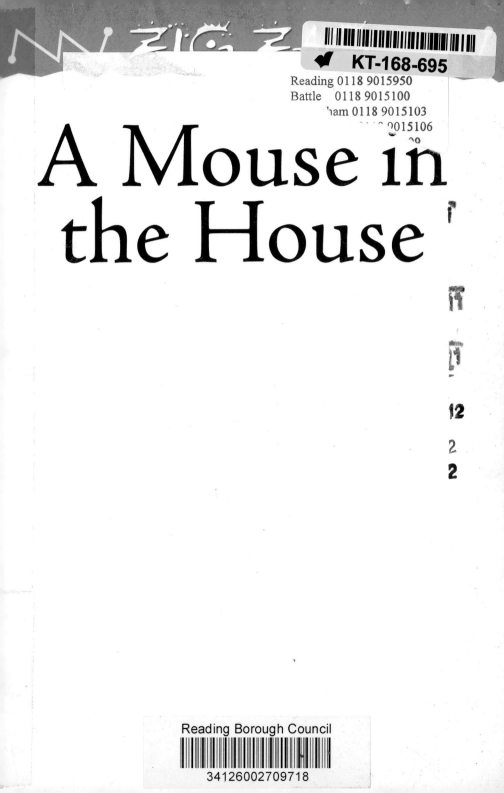

A Mouse in the House

First published 2007
Evans Brothers Limited
2A Portman Mansions
Chiltern St
London W1U 6NR

Text copyright © Vivian French 2007
Illustrations copyright © Tim Archbold 2007

British Library Cataloguing in Publication Data
French, Vivian
        A mouse in the house. - (Zig zag)
        1. Children's stories
        I. Title
        823.9'14[J]

ISBN-10: 0 237 53163 1 (hb)
13 digit ISBN: 978 0237 53163 8
ISBN-10: 0 237 53167 4 (pb)
13 digit ISBN: 978 0237 53167 6

Printed in China

Series Editor: Nick Turpin
Design: Robert Walster
Production: Jenny Mulvanny

A Mouse in the House

by Vivian French

illustrated by Tim Archbold

Evans

"Somebody help me,
help me, please…

There's a mouse in
my house…

…and it's eating my cheese!"

8

"Never mind, Gran – I've a cure for that. What you need is a black and white CAT!"

Where DID that cat go?

...horrible cheese-eating black and white mouse!"

14

"Don't worry, Gran, I know what to do. A big spotty DOG is the thing for you!"

"Oh no! Oh no!

Where DID that dog go?

All that I've got today
in my house…

…is a big and spotty
black and white mouse!"

"Don't worry Gran,
I know what to do…

...a dear little FLEA
is the thing for you."

"Three cheers! That mouse has scurried away.

There's only ME in my house today..."

"Somebody help me!
Help me, please –

I'm itching and scratching…

Why not try reading another ZigZag book?